Willard V. Huntington

Yesterday : A Poem

Willard V. Huntington

Yesterday : A Poem

ISBN/EAN: 9783744720991

Printed in Europe, USA, Canada, Australia, Japan

Cover: Foto ©Andreas Hilbeck / pixelio.de

More available books at **www.hansebooks.com**

YESTERDAY

Yesterday

A Poem

By

Willard V. Huntington

Illustrated By

Carll Dahlgren

San Francisco Cal.
The Bancroft Company
–1888~

I

An aged man, with mournful mien,

Moved slowly o'er the village green;

And as he paused, and looked around,

Upon this old familiar ground,

I thought I heard him sadly say:

" Alas! alas! my yesterday."

II

His form was bent with pressing years;

His face revealed the mark of tears;

His old-time garb was threadbare worn,

And made him look yet more forlorn;

As, leaning low upon his cane,

He seemed to speak those words again.

III

The children lingered on their way,
To see this stranger, old and gray;
And, marv'ling, asked themselves among:
"Could he have been, like us, once young?"
Then Wonder fled at Age distressed,
And Pity moved each infant breast.

"Oh! ancient man," quoth I, "I pray
Why mournest thou for yesterday?"

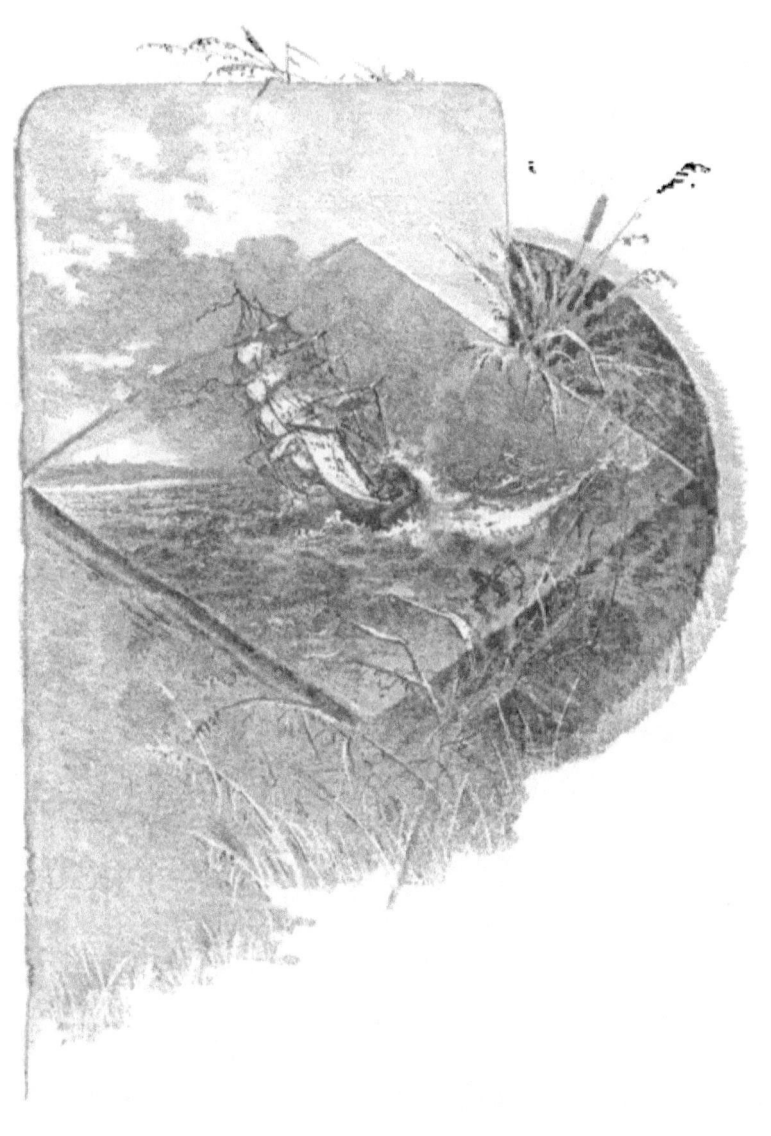

I V

"Wherefore," he said, "dost question me
In this—my last extremity?
For friends are few and seldom seen
Whene'er the storm clouds intervene;
But, let our bark outride the blast,
'Neath sunny skies her anchors cast,
And lo! to fickle impulse true,
With coming Fortune, friends come too.

V

" Where Indian spices freight the air

With fragrance ever sweet and rare,

I've seen each pleasant, peaceful isle

Adorned with Nature's fairest smile,

As though to all the world she'd say:

' Here will I take my holiday.'

Too quickly doth a hand, unseen,

Shut out this view and shift the scene

VI

" To Afric's shore—that torrid main.

Oh! hear'st thou not the hurricane!

Sprung from its lair in Libyan land,

Place of simoon and desert sand?

Again resounds the lion's roar

Upon that lonely, dismal shore;

Once more the warrior's battle cry

Up from the glade goes floating by.

VII

"Where Arctic frosts begirt the pole,

And make of it a phantom goal,

Whose mystery remains the same

As when this world from chaos came;

There, too, my fate hath taken me,

But to return—the wreck you see.

VIII

" Oft as a child my feet here strayed,

Among these trees I've sought the shade;

And here, rejoiced o'er school tasks done,

I've watched the setting of the sun,

Which seems not now so far away,

As when it marked that youthful day.

IX

" Ye peaceful hills! how fair to see—

Dear bound'ries of mine infancy;

Behold this early dwelling place

Forever locked in thine embrace;

When Life and Death here meet no more,

Still will ye watch the valley o'er.

X

" What voices low salute the ear

When Mem'ry bids the Past appear!

What forms and faces greet the eye,

And pass in quick succession by,

As homeward bound, from Learning's seat,

They throng each quiet village street!

XI

" Some wend their way, with idle speech;

Some, doth the book of Nature teach;

Some move in little groups apart,

As clannish instinct sways the heart,

And prompts thus early to define

The winding of each social line.

XII

" Some trick the old; with mock and jeer

Some wring from Age th' unwilling tear;

Some, of a gentler sex and mien,

Bring sweet Compassion to the scene;

Some smile, some sing an old-time song,

And others, heedless, pass along.

XIII

" With snow-clad ground in Winter's tide,

When merrily the sledges glide

O'er sun-lit jewels flashing there,

How quickly did we rout dull care!

Naught made our joy seem more complete

Than tinkling bells and prancing feet.

XIV

" By yonder brooklet's vernal brink,

How sings again the bobolink!

Sweet as the voice of one I knew,

Who sleeps so deep, beneath the dew—

E'en Nature's notes, in tones more dear,

Could never hope to reach her ear.

XV

" How happy sped the summer-time

With harvest song throughout our clime!

Again the reapers drift afield ;

Again the golden banners yield ;

The sturdy strokes, firm dealt and slow,

Soon lay each bearded army low.

XVI

" And then came Autumn in the train,

    With ripened fruit and groaning wain;

    So full she looked of coming cheer,

    One scarce could note the dying year;

    But, ever thus, it seems to me,

    Few pleasures free from pain can be.

XVII

"In yonder tree-embowered street,

    Of turf bereft by passing feet,

    There is a cottage, small and old,

    Whose hearth, once bright, has long been cold;

    Each window then revealed at night

    A welcome home in ev'ry light;

    But now, that I have ceased to roam,

    I find, for me, no light—no home

XVIII

" My mother, standing at the door

    To watch me thence, I'll see no more;

    There did my father daily strive,

    And vainly hope, anew, to thrive;

    Until, with burdens overcome,

    He, too, has sought another home.

XIX

" Down in the churchyard's hallowed nook,

Fast by the ever-flowing brook,

There, 'neath the willow and the yew,

All whom I loved are lost to view.

Then, marvel not, that I should say:

Alas! alas! my yesterday."

X X

Thus did he speak, and went his way;

Each silent bird resumed its lay;

The breeze, all hushed in sympathy,

Again communed with ev'ry tree,

And, whisp'ring low, still seems to say:

" Alas! alas! my yesterday."